DIRECTORY

CHRISTOPHER LINFORTH

Directory

OTIS BOOKS
MFA WRITING PROGRAM
Otis College of Art and Design
LOS ANGELES 2020

Book design and typesetting: Jenna Dorian

ISBN-13: 978-9980-2-4305-8

OTIS BOOKS
MFA WRITING PROGRAM
Otis College of Art and Design
9045 Lincoln Boulevard
Los Angeles, CA 90045

https://www.otis.edu/mfa-writing/otis-books
otisbooks@otis.edu

For the living and the dead

Contents

Directory

Back when we loved our mother, we recorded her telephone calls. Most nights she took the handset into the bath and talked to her string of men. We sat downstairs next to the speaker, Dictaphone in hand, copying the sounds of her voice. She spoke of stripping off her leather skirt, her silk blouse and rainbow fishnets. She laughed about not wearing any underwear. She joked about the bubbles in the bath, the placement of her loofah. The men spluttered, asked her to keep going, provide more details. They always wanted to know more. Our mother acted coy. She said she had long tanned legs, freshly shaven–the men would not believe how smooth her skin felt. When pushed, she described her breasts, the pinkness of her nipples. Then she would splash about, top off the bath with steaming water. Her skin pruned; her makeup ran; her hairpiece slopped into the soapy water behind her neck. We heard breaths deepen, become intertwined, smoky. A last guttural moan and the call would be over. Water channeled down the pipes, out of the house, to the sewer. Our mother would emerge towel-clad, wanting us to fetch her a strong drink, but we'd escape to the basement, the cot behind the tool rack, and split up: one hidden beneath the sheets, the other on top. We had committed the conversations to memory and liked to replay them as man and woman, swapping roles every night. When the handset returned to the cradle, we crept up the stairs and sneaked into the living room to watch our mother dialing another man.

Listing

Our parents obliterated us.

Back then we had names. But they are gone now.

Our former selves no longer exist.

We are American and un-American.

We are fragments of our personal archives.

Silently adrift in our insular world.

The architecture of language surrounds us.

But we wish to run away.

And explore the cities and towns of this nation.

And consume and regurgitate.

We want to discover who we were and will be.

We read Marx and Freud and slog through Aristotle and Plotinus.

We adore Walter Benjamin. Or, at least, one of his ideas.

We laugh at our PTSD diagnosis.

We have lived through K-holes and sad comedowns from Molly.

We are fuckups and weirdos.

And we lie constantly.

But then the people who know us will not be surprised.

We are two, sometimes three.

We fetishize telephones and compilations of their numbers.

We desire men and women on the other end of the line.

We become these men and women, boys and girls; we occupy nebulous pronouns in between.

We inhabit every point on the spectrum.

We confess rarely.

But today is different.

Gestalt

Our misdeeds–let's start with those. We made our old man piss his pants. He limped away, sopped the urine with a kitchen rag and kept his hand over his crotch. He swore at us, said we were no good since our mother left. We laughed. We didn't care. We filched his bottom-shelf vodka and terrorized the neighborhood, rode our dirt bikes up and down the road, burning rubber outside of Mrs. Macomber's house. She watched us from her bedroom window. Her flash of silvery hair a clear sign we had her spooked. We stole her underwear from the drying line, strung it to the back of our bikes, saw if it worked as a parachute. The panties flew away, ripped, busted, left in the street for everyone to see. She came out, threatened to tell our old man. Go ahead, we said. He cares less than we do. Mrs. Macomber raised her fist, her knotted fingers thin and brittle. She wanted to punch us, knock us out, teach us a lesson. We rode up her pristine lawn, stepped off our bikes, stood in front of her. We jutted out our chins. Take your best shot, we said. She fell to her knees. She cried about her flowerbed. We had destroyed her African daisies and her purple-blue phlox with our tires. She clutched the stems of her plants and tried to replant them; we hopped on our bikes, left her crying in the dirt. She died a few weeks later. Our old man said she tripped in her garden, broke her hip, developed septicemia. DNR.

We're really here to talk about our virtues. Ten years ago, we slunk out of our old man's house. We sped our dirt bikes out of town, down 84. Rumor had it our mother was shacked up with a man in Fishkill. We rolled along Main Street, eyeing any woman around forty. Any woman who seemed she'd had twin boys and abandoned them. A saggy belly, lopsided breasts, shellacked blonde hair–this is what we looked for. We propped our bikes against the picture window of a laundromat and searched inside, then moved on to the clothing stores, the churches, the solitary teahouse. We questioned women, asked if they knew who we were. The women feigned ignorance. We slapped our chests and pointed to the color of our eyes. We match, we said. You match too. The women glanced around, crossed the street, dialed cellphones. We ignored their fright and carried on with our quest. Inside a florist's, we stole a bouquet of hydrangea and white roses from the wedding display. We lugged the flowers all through a clapboard neighborhood. At the end of one cul-de-sac, a man stood talking to a woman. She was our mother, she had to be, and he resembled Mrs. Macomber's son. He had the same silver hair, the squashed nose. One of us tackled the man, sent him to the ground, and the other pressed the bouquet on our mother. She smiled at us. That was enough. We ran back to our bikes. We rode south then west a little, finally hitting the City. So perhaps we don't have virtues. But surely we have something.

Lecture

Our father tells us the French word for peephole is *judas.* He bears down on us, angles his pinky toward his eye. The betrayer is the size of my pupil, he says. Sometimes smaller. We don't reply. We let him drone on about the Bible, about respecting your father, staying out of his business. We don't know what any of this has to do with the French language. *Quelle*? we say. Our father's cheeks redden, his chest swells. He turns around, and we follow him into the hallway. He rummages through the closet and brings out a roll of black tape. He snaps off a piece and sticks it over the front door's peephole. See? he says. Now come here. We step forward and he tears off several more pieces of tape. He presses the tape over our eyes. We hear him walk down the hall and enter his bedroom. His muffled voice seems to be directed to someone else now. Maybe he guesses about understanding our spy game; the mission our mother gave us to identify his lover. We peel off the tape. Our eyelids burn but the pain is worth it. We slip inside the hall closet and keep the door ajar. Two loud voices echo through the house. Then they go quiet. Through our watery eyes, we see a strange man open the front door and run toward his car.

Rope Trick

To prove our love, we strung the tightrope across the backyard. We climbed on at opposite ends. The boughs of the two elms sagged with our weight. We steadied ourselves against the trunks and goaded each other to go first. Neither of us would let go of the branches above. Our love, if it had ever existed, evaporated. We were two boys. Two boys at a stalemate.

Only one of us knew whose backyard this was. That one of us boys was the nephew of the owner. The other boy lived across town, in a small apartment with his mother. She had little knowledge of her son's desire for the other boy. She found her son aloof, uninterested in the things a boy his age should like. Both of us had heard her confess this concern to her family. Both of us had dismissed it.

We'd met at our high school's Circus Club. We cemented our friendship over failed attempts to juggle and lob foam pies at cardboard faces. The club president kicked us out. We were glad. We told him we were starting a Daredevil Club. We would one-up that doe-eyed killjoy. Late afternoons, we flung darts at squirrels, jumped off one-story rooftops, made the crazed neighborhood pit bull chase us.

We were still at a stalemate when the owner of the land approached the tightrope. He knew one of us was his nephew, but he didn't let on. He drew a knife from the leather holster on his belt and staggered to the middle of the rope. He glanced each way, then gripped the rope, pressed the blade against the braided sisal. He offered us a final chance to get off. We stayed silent, and he began to cut. As the rope frayed, we glanced at each other, felt love rekindled. We outstretched our arms, placed one foot in front of the other, and ran along the tightrope to the center as fast as we could.

Cul-de-Sac

In the backyard, firecrackers fizz in our hands. We dare each other to throw first. We draw the firecrackers to our mouths, chomp on them like cigars. Watch the fuses burn. Blue smoke drifts up our noses, down our throats. We hold the smoke inside of us, blackening our lungs, exhaling when we feel sick. Then we hear the gruff voice of our neighbor and the snarl of his dog. He threatens to call our parents, CPS, the police. As we withdraw the firecrackers from our mouths, they bang. Fine gray powder coats our still-intact fingers. We laugh and throw the charred remains over the fence. Our neighbor peers over the top rail; his domed forehead gleams in the midday sun. We know he is on tiptoes, even standing on a brick. Where are your mom and dad? he asks. They are gone, but we do not let on. They left days ago. A trip, they said. To visit relatives. They didn't fool us – our family is close with no one. Our parents always said that was our fault. But we care little for what our neighbors think about us. This is our neighborhood, our street; we decide what we do here. We light more firecrackers, wave them above our heads. Our neighbor steps back, disappears from view. We lob the firecrackers over the fence, hear them explode in midair. An animal whimpers, then a soft voice speaks. We lie in the grass, try to glimpse our neighbor through the gap at the bottom of the fence. In the dirt lies a mound of tan fur. The retriever lolls on its side, legs shaking unnaturally, its watery black eyes rolled back. Our neighbor hunches over his dog, drives the brick into its skull.

Initiation

We swiped at the boy's surgical mask. We grazed the smooth surface, felt the hole in his face where his upper lip should have been. He ducked and weaved, bobbed away from our clumsy attack. His thin body was lanky and elastic, could dance around us with no trouble. Straps lassoed from the mask to the back of his head. The knots looked doubled, tripled, so many twists and loops that the straps would never untie. One of us caught his shirt and pulled him over. He stood in the middle of us, raised his hands, egged us on. Three on one – we liked our odds. We had a bag of peaches, ripe and swollen, and we each took a single fruit. One of us lobbed a peach at the boy's face, hitting his forehead square, sending him off-balance. He wobbled as he dodged the next one. We caught his wrist, then tackled him to the ground. All three of us sat on him: his legs, his waist, his chest. He shifted beneath us. We dug our fingertips under the mask's fabric, past the nose down into the hole. Eat a peach, we said, pressing one into the mask. The boy didn't speak. He shook his head. We leaned back, tore the mask from his face, snapping the elastic straps. We rose, carrying our prize, passing it from one to the other. The boy finally stood. We saw the crescent of dark space, a mouth above a mouth. He took the last peach from the bag. His half-mouth slid over the furred surface, his bottom teeth held the peach in place. He slurped the fruit, breaking its skin. He devoured the sweet flesh and spat the stone back at us.

Ceremony

We chant his name from the clifftop. Far below, our father cranes his neck for the source of the noise. We call out to him again, then collapse in the undergrowth, laughing. We pick up stones and judge our father's position. He's naked in his deckchair, a newspaper in his lap, the gray sea in front of him. We each pitch a stone – one skitters across a tide pool, way off; the other slugs the back of his chair. Our father thuds forward and stands, hand stretched around to the soft skin between his shoulder blades. His head dips. We hear a cry. We feel a strange pleasure; we become erect, and we grope for more stones. We hurl several limestone shards as far as we can. One catches his temple. We duck, then spring up again. Over the cliff edge, we see our father sprawled on the coarse sand. A red welt has ballooned across his back and blood smears the side of his face. We chant Father, Father, Father. Waves foam across the shore toward his head. Water touches his thinning hair. He doesn't flinch or jerk. We scramble down the cliff and gather up pieces of rock, lay them over his body, slowly cover his flesh. Seawater runs over the rocks, channels down the crevices, blessing him as only nature can do.

Recoil

The voice called to us in late winter. Our names echoed across the hoarfrosted grass to where the two of us stood in front of our childhood home. We could barely look at the peeling shingles or the collapsed roof. Through the broken window, we peered inside our former bedroom. Three of us once shared an area of ten by ten feet. A triple bunkbed sat against the far wall; we'd needed a ladder to reach the highest bunk, where a boy could scarcely fit, let alone a father. Often two bodies squeezed into that top bunk, so close to each other in the dark, they could hear their breath ricochet off the ceiling, the warm puffs of air, of muffled *yes* and *no*. We could all hear; we tried to mask the sounds with our pillows. But the voices grew louder: *Don't cry. Be a man. Stop.* Sometimes, he would work his way down the bunkbeds, saying he loved us. Whether this was true hardly matters anymore. Back then we believed him. We believed everything until that telephone call saved us. He left our bedroom when the phone rang that night. When he scooped up the receiver, thunder shook the house. The single shot from the hunting rifle split the back of his head, voided any love, any concern or guilt for what he had done. We had never wanted an apology, just to be left alone. And he did, in the end, thanks to the youngest of us, a lost presence in our lives. Now, in front of the house, we listen again to the voice of the missing one: a cry for the three of us to be reunited.

Dinner

At that time in our lives, we rose at dusk for the feeding shift. Still in our underwear, we crept downstairs and into the kitchen. Shiny black bugs skittered across the tile floor. The lazy cockroaches remained on the counter and in the tinfoil containers stinking of rotten noodles; a few silvery beetles disappeared into the seal of the refrigerator. In the living room our mother railed at the television, at the caregiver exiting the house. We heard calls for dinner, thuds on the floor, shouts for our dead father. We rubbed crust from our eyes, then surveyed the leftovers on the floor: the cartons of moldy coleslaw, the potatoes sitting in an old washing machine drum. Our mother wanted something to ease the eternal pain in her stomach. She cried about it every evening, said it was caused by our father's death. His coronary was our fault, she claimed. Even now, we could hear her saying that he had despised us, that raising twins had broken his spirit. He had spiraled into his own world; he desired food, every bit of it in the house, and she now carried on his legacy. We pawed through the cabinets, then the refrigerator. We slapped a slab of raw chicken on a plate, sprinkled blue crystal salts onto the pinkish skin. We slipped into the living room, saw our mother's bulbous silhouette. The television flashed commercials: fat burgers and buttered shrimp. She jabbed at the remote control. The volume ramped up. The bass rumbled through her chairside buckets of seed packets, the fruit crates stuffed with newspapers and women's magazines. Dolls toppled off the bookshelves. Her possessions were part of her, she enjoyed saying, but we were not. She yelled for us to hurry. We looked at the slimy chicken breast again, second-guessed the blue crystals. Our mother's favorite gameshow came on the television and she roared for her food. We'd had enough. We sneaked closer to her. Ammonia stung our noses. Beside the foot of her recliner sat a line of soda bottles filled with urine. A string of Christmas lights lay around the bottles, around the skirt of her chair. We cooed: Mamma, Mamma, Mamma. We offered her the plate and she snatched it from us. Leave, she said. I want to enjoy this. She used to say she was a proud mother. She used to look to see what she was eating.

Date Night

In the bathroom, our babysitter comes at us with tincture of benzoin. She unscrews the lid and holds the glass bottle above her head. The amber liquid swishes inside, spills over the lip. We cower behind the shower curtain. I see you, she says. As she pulls back the curtain, we turn the showerhead her way, spray her face with steaming hot water. Our babysitter shrieks that she will call our parents. She hates that we're twins, but not twins, the pair of us almost identical to strangers. Our spindly bodies look pale, rarely exposed to the outside world. We hop out of the bath and surge past her. We hear her footfalls as she follows. We dive into our parents' room and jump onto the bed. Our babysitter snatches our ankles, trips the pair of us onto the coverlet. Our parents' odor puffs into the air – all three of us can smell the stink of our stepfather's semen, our mother's sweat, the cheap hairspray she overuses every morning. Our parents always rut after returning from their Saturday night dinner. They carry in leftovers, a bottle of late-night supermarket wine; they pay the babysitter with a check, call her a taxi. Tell her to go. They smack us when we refuse to sleep. They leave bruises on our arms and chests. Tonight, before they left, our mother egged on our stepfather. She told him we did not view him as our father. He threw us to the floor and slapped us around, his class ring nicking our cheeks. We blamed the cat when the babysitter arrived. She asked to see the tabby, which died years ago. We don't remember its name. Now our babysitter wrinkles her nose. Enough, she snaps. She climbs onto the bed. She hunches over and tips the bottle of benzoin onto a wad of tissue. She dabs at our arms, cleans up a little blood. Then she moves onto the second of us. We brace for the pain. Now stay still, she says. This will toughen you up.

Belief

On the day we flee town, we will want the neighborhood to know what happened. We will tell stories about our stepfather to the kind and not-so-kind men on our street, to the cops who size us up to see if we are underage, turning tricks, will turn a trick with them. We will run door-to-door and confess to the rumors circulating in town. We will bypass the churches, the mosque and synagogue, and the community center run by our stepfather. We will tell everything about him: his good works fundraising for the school, his organization of the Maypole dance to reintroduce the values of the Natural World, his insistence on an order of things. Men above women–he voiced that belief many times. The tales of incest are false. Or possibly half-true. Either way, what he did to us will come out. We will see to that. We will leave this place, go find our mother. Some time ago she drove west, to Montana or Wyoming. Her goodbye note promised freedom there, a wild landscape of mountains and ranges. A place without our stepfather. Our mother didn't want much. Just somewhere she could be safe. When she fled, she told no one. She slipped away, rode a Greyhound, hitchhiked across several states, found a cabin in the woods. Her return to nature only spurred our stepfather's beliefs, in using us as surrogate wives. This act was not religious, though he was zealous, a believer in himself and his place in the universe. He read up on obscure branches of Mormonism, the practices of Seventh-day Adventists, the intricacies of Kabbalah and Jainism. He seemed to prefer, even espouse, a mishmash of ideas: vows of silence and chastity for women. He said we were equal to the dust on the floor. He pushed these practices on us; he wanted us quiet; he wanted us to be his. We will never forget his rough skin, his bloated potbelly, his greasy silver hair. We can never erase the burn of him inside of us. Silence has lived in our house, in our neighborhood, all through this town. Our voice boxes are warming up, our bodies flexing, charged with new energy. Any day now we will shout.

Tongues

In the beginning, we thought our stepfather knew our language. We spoke to him, pleaded with him, asked him to leave us alone. We thought he understood. We left home at sixteen. He followed us to Wichita, to Tallahassee, to Milwaukee. He waited outside our new apartments, his reddened cheeks, his slicked hair, his sour odor giving him away. He called after us, begged for us to stop, come back to him. You're my girls, he said. We yelled: Rape! Fire! Murder! Anything to make the neighbors notice. His body lumbered toward us, fighting the stiffness of his muscles, his shot heart. We sister-pledged to each other this would be the last time. We were stupid and desperate. We split up, hoping to lose our stepfather. One to L.A., the other to Sedona. We checked in daily, ordered locks and alarm systems, memorized long activation codes. We kept pepper sprays in our pocketbooks, stowed Tasers in the glovebox. We laxed over the years. When we talked we spoke of daycare, morning iced coffee, yoga in the afternoon. Our once-long stretches of conversation blinked away to birthday greetings and holiday plans. A final New Year, a millennium celebration, brought our stepfather back. He tracked us to a beach house in Malibu, waited until our husbands took the girls for ice cream, then asked for a welcoming kiss. He dipped his head and planted his lips upon ours. His familiar sour smell, his days-old beard, his rough skin, all sickened us. One of us offered him a tour, the other slunk away to the kitchen. I'd like to see the bedroom, he said. We took him to the master suite. He idled by the bed, smoothing the sheets. We asked him to turn around, face us. Close your eyes, we said, watching him do so. Now say you're sorry. Our stepfather started to rant, but he never saw the kitchen knife that sliced his tongue. The wad of pink flesh tumbled to the cream carpet. Ears followed, two puckered pieces of cartilage. He spoke something, in the end, but we do not know what he said.

Reunion

We never thought he would say Amen. A life without us and that's all he said in the end. Thirty-eight years separate our child selves from the adults watching our stepfather die. His pale body is a testament to his time in a long-stay motel, to his vaporized liver, to his packs of Natural American Spirit. Cigarettes lie on the bedside table–loosies purchased from a man he knows, a man he owes money to. He owes us a childhood, a good life for our mother. She is gone but we remember her counsel: Don't believe your stepfather. On the videotape he speaks that one word, then a nurse enters the room, checks the pulse on his wrist, his neck. She places her hand above his mouth. His eyes fix to a point in midair, a place where his channel of breath left the Amen. A soundwave–now long attenuated–is still a soundwave we can hear. The word still echoes through us, burns us, lets us know he was thinking of only himself at the end: a coda to his life. We watch the video of his death from thousands of miles away. We watch together, two sisters, in the same room for the first time in a decade. Our husbands talk upstairs, care for our boys and girls, drink craft beers, catch up on other family news. We stand in front of the television. We barely recognize our stepfather, though neither of us will admit it. We know it must be him: his thatch of gray hair, his dull blue eyes, his knotted fists that felled us. He says nothing on the tape apart from the word. There's hope in us that he means something else by it. No priest stands over him, no Bible rests by his cigarettes, no sign of the cross or last rites uttered by the nurse. We rewind the video. Watch it again and again: Amen, Amen, Amen.

Elegy

Mayflies hatched along the river running by our house. The winged insects flew over the water in great billowing swarms; we watched rainbow trout devour a few close to the surface. The sky blushed mauve above us. It was dusk, and we still loved our mother then.

We encased our hands with hers and led her to the bank. We found mayfly molts and collected the ghost skins in our shirttails. We rushed our find downriver to the circle of stones. We piled the molts and enclosed them with branches. We poured a little of our mineral spirit over the pyre, and before she lit the match, she suggested a prayer.

We could think of no words that fit the moment.

Our mother dropped the match and studied the bright little flame. Let's remember his death, she said.

Procedure

The PICC line sits flush against her arm. We watch the nurse slide the catheter into our mother's cephalic vein, probe deeper inside of her. Our mother, swaddled in hospital white, looks away from her body. Her gray eyes lock with ours. Progeny, she always calls us. Not children or kids or daughters, but progeny. At home, she curated our education: mammalian anatomy, set theory, metaphysics, Theosophy. The basement served as our classroom. Tacked to the walls were photographs of notable Slavic triplets. Dark-haired Russian girls directed their glares at us. Our mother instructed us on how to be notable, how to present superiority. Challenge others, she said. Show them Truth. She taught us to ignore men and lesser women, to be committed to the cause. Disciples, she called us, when she forgot we were her progeny. On some days, she didn't know who or what we were. She had reduced our relationship to a hierarchical binary. She was object *o* and we were set *A*. She broadcast this theory to everyone in the neighborhood, to the operator on the emergency line. When the ambulance came for her, she spouted about the von Neumann universe, declared the EMTs were less than zero. Outside of her hospital room, our fingers splay on the glass. The catheter rests in her superior vena cava, skirting her right auricula. She complains to the nurse; she feels a sharp pain; she curses the nurse's clumsy insertion. Doctors appear, whip our mother away, the gurney heading toward Radiology. We run behind. We await the X-rays. We want to decipher the grayscale film–look for her heart.

Timber

The tree fell on our mother. A neighbor identified it as a lodgepole pine. He was an expert, so he claimed, said he once worked as an arborist. He wore coveralls and a leather tool belt; his workman boots were dull and scuffed. He stood next to the tree and scratched his thick beard. Our mother was silent; only a stiff hand visible. The neighbor axed off the branches, sawed the trunk into neat circles. Wafer-thin slices he sold as flying discs, replacements for vinyl. He hawked pine needles as mementos of our mother. She wouldn't have minded, the neighbor told us, she was always fond of that tree. For as long as we could remember, our mother had never mentioned the lodgepole pine. She seldom left the house or chatted with strangers. Still, it was a fine tree. We helped the neighbor carve a casket from the heartwood. Together we lowered her body into the smooth vessel. We applied layers of black varnish, a final waterproof lacquer. The neighbor said it resembled a torpedo. We felt honored. Our father had been a Marine. We knew little else about him. Years before the tree incident, our mother just liked to tell us he had been at sea. A sailor, a Lance Corporal, a machine-gunner – the story changed, yet somehow remained the same. The neighbor listened to our stories as we launched the casket into the river. Our mother floated away, back toward the ocean. We called after her as loud as we could, let the people know she was coming.

Visitation

Her death–let's put that aside for now. We were road-tripping south, through the Carolinas, across Georgia and Alabama, trying to reach Oklahoma. Our aunt, a self-proclaimed mystic, was said to hold séances in the front room of her Tulsa house. We had never met the woman but heard stories about her from our old man: one-eyed, bald, rosary beads around her neck, lesbian. Always malt-liquor drunk. Our old man seldom said a kind word about her. Or about anybody.

Past West Memphis, the car was almost out of gas. We stopped at a highway motel and rented a room, sharing a bed like the old days. We drained our water bottles and snacked on the last of our peppered jerky. At the window, we studied the road, the hundreds of miles still to go before Tulsa. We used the motel phone to call our aunt. She answered with surprise in her voice, unsure of who we were. I didn't know I had nephews, she said. We told her our old man liked to keep us a secret. She kept quiet, so we confessed: We want to speak to our mother.

The two of us sat cross-legged, facing each other on the bed, our hands clasped together. The phone receiver rested between us. Our aunt chanted a few words, fake Chinese or something like it, repeating the string of nonsense over and over. We considered hanging up, forgetting about this awful road trip. Then our aunt stopped. We bowed our heads, listening to her faint breath. A new woman's voice came from the speaker and we pressed our ears into the plastic handset as hard as we could.

Pitstop

We blitzed through Oklahoma, finally stopping at a gas station in Slapout. In this slice of the state, a town in name only, we pumped gas into our stolen SUV, then dashed inside the connected mini-mart and ignored the clerk's welcome. We fixed ourselves a couple of slushies and a pair of caramel-syrup coffees, laughing about double-fisting the drinks. We picked up some bison jerky and microwaved two mystery meat sandwiches. Every sign in the store had the town's name printed on it. *Don't Stay Long, Slapout!* said T-shirts, bubble stickers, car decals, beer koozies. We didn't get the joke; we didn't even care. This was Oklahoma. When we stuck candy bars in our pockets, the clerk came over. He asked us to pay, then leave. The man, barely older than us, had the name Jim stitched onto his shirt pocket. We feigned ignorance and he pointed to the convex mirror above us. Game's up, he said. Before Slapout, before Lovejoy and Bacon Level, before even Fishkill, we had dealt with small-town men like Jim. We had dealt with Bowling Shirt Eric and the contractor we called Mike the Mouthguard. At the Georgia-Alabama border we had run into perma-tanned Larry. His thinning hair and bulbous eyes didn't stop his anecdotes about the women who loved him. Maddi was the sweetest truck-stop girl of all, he'd said. We humored him, but only for a short time. When we gave Larry a choice of coming with us, he brought out the miniature Magic 8 Ball on his keychain. Every time he shook the ball, the answer came up: *Outlook not so good.* And it wasn't. Not for Larry, or Mike, or Eric. Now Jim had the same dilemma. Stay or leave with us. Jim had little choice, really. He stank of dope, of community college, of failure to leave a town of two residents–just him and his dad. His shirt was too big for him, his black khakis too tight. Whoever this man was, he was not Jim. Maybe he was Jim Jr. or Jim III. But he was not simply Jim. His dad, First Jim, owned the shirt, probably lived in the trailer out back, fashioned the tourist Slapout nonsense with a friend-of-a-friend in China, or some local factory with a digital printer. Either way, we weren't buying. We tailed Son of Jim to the counter, waited for him to go around to the other side. We handed him an empty plastic bag for the cash. Now it was his turn to pretend not to know what was happening. Time to become someone else, we said.

Apocrypha

At the rear of our new house we waited for moonrise. While the sun neared the horizon, we sketched the elderly neighbor. He was edging himself up a wooden extension ladder, a portable oxygen tank strapped to his back. He was in denim overalls, worn white on the buttocks, pant legs unevenly cuffed. With each step, his shoulders rose, his lungs inflating with vital air. It took him a long time to reach the top. Once there, his arm stretched to the steel bars crisscrossing the attic porthole. He fiddled with a key in the lock, faltering, finally able to swing open the metal lattice. Then he peered inside the darkened window.

We called to our neighbor, asked him to turn around so we could capture a true likeness of his face. He lifted his foot off the rung; his torso twisted in our direction. Below his silky white hair, blankness dulled his eyes. We erased his rictus expression and redrew his face, then waved our sketchpads above our heads. Our neighbor turned back to the ladder and clutched the side rail. His body trembled, his vibrations wobbling the ladder. We rose from our deckchairs and hurried to his backyard. We hopped the picket fence, sped across his lawn, reached the bottom of the ladder just in time. We pressed our weight against the base. We glanced up and asked if he was all right.

There's someone in the attic, he said.

A man or a woman? we asked.

Too dark to see which.

Can we look?

Go in through the house.

Stay still, we said, and you won't fall.

He gave off a strange huff, almost a laugh, but closer to a cry. We saluted him but he did not salute back. We entered the house through the backdoor. The kitchen had been stripped of appliances. Only a camping stove stood atop a side table. Canned goods were arranged by food group: vegetable, meat, dessert. The swollen cans appeared old, spiked with *Clostridium botulinum.*

Along the hall, we peered into one of the rooms. Rows of dated bottles brimmed with liquids of a yellowed rainbow: washed-out vanilla to rich amber. The burning stench of ammonia soured the air. We ducked out, gladly, sickened by that fatherly odor. As we climbed the stairs, we assumed the old man was poor and riddled with Alzheimer's or the weird end of Obsessive-Compulsive Disorder. Since we had moved into the neighborhood, we had not seen him. Or anyone. In truth, we had failed to introduce ourselves to any of our neighbors. Perhaps, like us, they spent much of their time reading esoteric texts, hunting for obscure books online, or listening on the telephone to the advice of ex-literature professors, their ruminations on Russian novelists.

At the top of the house, we stopped in front of the attic door. The thick wooden door had a burnished silver knob. We twisted the stiff knob and heaved our shoulders against the solid oak panel; the two of us fell into the room, landing on the hardwood floor. The door closed. We were trapped in darkness. We scurried across the floor to a faint shining circle on the far side of the attic. The glass in the porthole had been tinted, smoked to opaquest black. As our eyes adjusted, we could make out a schoolroom desk, a sheaf of labels and a single pen on top. By the foot of the desk sat a collection of glass bottles and jugs of drinking water.

We went to the window. Our neighbor loomed on the

other side – a great shadow, stocky, muscular. His change in stature absolved him of his age, of his urine collection.

There's no one in here, we said.

Spit hit the glass, followed by his rebuttal: I see a couple of artists. Then, with ease, he maneuvered the web of metal bars back in front of the window.

What are you doing? We're neighbors.

I don't live here, he said.

He saluted us and his silhouette disappeared from our view. We could hear the slap of his boots as he shinnied back down. We rapped on the glass, then punched the pane until it cracked and shattered into pieces. Our knuckles were sliced, bruised, strangely numb. Pale light shafted into the attic. We kneeled before the window; we saw a crescent moon in the sky.

Folktale

We think about the sound of the word *aubade*. We say it as one syllable, then two. We paint the sound as light and rhythm, as the breath of a sleeping woman.

We debate the differences between an aubade and an alba. We do it slowly, considering whether her dream brings forth a lover.

We read Hoffmann's story "The Sandman" in German. We speak the words close to the canvas.

We gesso over the last block of color.

We dot the stretcher bar with cut squares of tape and press the bar against the wall. We hold it for a second, drawing on muscle-memory and the memory of holding her, then let the stretcher bar fall.

We photograph the studio. We photograph the glass jar of turpentine. We photograph the tear of skin on her foot arch and the acrylic drips and the face of the man who sings at the window.

We listen to the man's melodic plea.

We interpret his words as a dead-star constellation. We use a thumbtack to pierce holes in the dark areas of the painting.

We go outside and confront the man. We ask him if the woman ever woke up.

Father's Day

In the middle of the heatwave we slaughter the goats. We hold the animals down, knees pressed to their shoulders, fingers keeping the heads still. We spike the sticking knives through their necks, behind their jawbones, quieting their bleating. Blood seeps into the dry dirt. Goat eyes blink to glass. We show our sons how to gut the insides, scoop out the hearts and livers, remove the kidneys and the layers of white fat. They watch us run skinning knives from the animals' ankles to the anuses, across bellies to the thickly muscled necks. We tug off the hides, angle our blades against the fatty flesh. When we hack off the goat heads, our sons ask questions about goat-spirits, about the disappearance of their mothers. The women had left us when the heatwave began. At dusk, they had buried their heartjars in the earth and walked away. A line of women, mothers and wives, drifted through the valley. They sacrificed themselves for the men and boys, for the warriors left among us. Our sons ask for details, ask what heartjars are, ask if we're telling the truth or if their mothers abandoned us all. We slap goat hocks against our boys' chests, order them to carry the meat to the fire. Dark blood stains the boys' skin. Ages them. They skewer the veined slabs on long iron rods, stake the goat remains vertically all around the firepit. They watch the meat, turn it periodically, shout to us when the flesh is charred. Then we descend upon the firepit. We devour hunks of goat. We feel the charge of vitality, of goat-spirits inside us. Our boys circle away from the firepit, dig up the earth, hunting for the heartjars. The night's bruised light halts their search, and the boys migrate to the valley, follow the footprints their mothers left behind.

The Temple

We prayed for our lives to change. Then the pastor moved into our neighborhood and took over a run-down tenement in Alphabet City. He brought with him a dozen men, followers who recorded his every utterance with Dictaphones, then transcribed his words into pamphlets with titles like *Holy Man Speaks* and *The Collected Lists*, selling them for $9.95 in Tompkins Square Park.

Trucks arrived. Twelve men in radiation suits unloaded crates that were smooth and black, a muffled buzzing sound coming from within. Once from our window we saw them drop a crate. The corner fractured and a clear substance oozed out. One of the men knelt to clean up the mess with an old newspaper; the text disappeared as he mopped the liquid into a nearby drain.

During the second week the tenement windows were boarded up, eight stories patched with thick lumber, nailed in by new workers who wore facemasks that resembled the pastor. We counted a dozen men, twelve visions of the pastor's serene expression, a kind of superior contentment. After the men finished and took down the scaffold, they went into the building and never came out.

After a month or so, as the fall leaves turned an odd shade of oxblood, strange sounds came from inside the building. Drilling, we thought, or maybe gunshots, went on for hours at a time. Government officials, with ID badges and clipboards, came and then left with thick books that weren't Bibles. At night panhandlers stopped by, looking for a free meal. They entered as if the place was just another soup kitchen or hostel. They left with expressions of fear. Their eyes bulged and their bodies flinched as though they had epilepsy or Parkinson's.

At the end of December, we could hear the New Year countdown from Times Square. On the shout of one, the brick walls of the tenement came down like the Biblical Jericho. A plume of dust mushroomed into the sky. As the view cleared, we saw a shining monolith. Smooth black tiles reflected the fireworks exploding over the city. From the building's grand archway, the pastor came out in lush robes of gold and silver and crossed the street to look back at his temple. His expression seemed still and plastic, as though he was wearing a mask of his own face.

The temple was the start of the area's gentrification. The neighborhood changed. People came to live here just so they could stare at the building. Residents remarked that it healed their ailments and made their stock portfolios rise. We couldn't afford the rent anymore, and we moved away to an apartment in Queens. Yet the other day we saw through our binoculars twelve new men enter the temple with steel picks and industrial jackhammers and not leave.

Chattel

The man points to the grain scale. He heaves each of us onto the cast-iron platform. We are young and plump. Or so he tells us. The three of us face the moon-shaped dial. The needle flickers up to our tri-weight. The man tries to read the number, but he cannot see through our huddled bodies. He prods us with his telescopic pointer. Stand back, he says. As he lunges forward, slashing the air, light flashes off the pointer's chrome finish. We sway and dodge; we attempt to swat it away. The man shuffles in the sawdust. Dust motes stick to his glistening scalp, his bare chest, his veined forearms pulsing in the heat. Make room, he says. He places one foot on the rim of the grain scale and leans forward, his arms outstretched toward us. We snatch away the pointer, whip it against his ribs and thick neck. The man falls back and then tries to join us again. We thrash his chest, then stab the pointer tip into his eyes. He drops to his knees and gropes for the edge of the platform. The needle shifts with his weight and we tread on his fingers. He yips in pain and lets go. He tells us he'll flay our skins for that. Then a group of grizzled men barge through the barn doors and stalk over to the grain scale. They glance at the dial and down to the man. They force a meat hook in his mouth, piercing the roof. They drag him out of the barn, out to be sold at the market.

Masterpiece

Our grandfather loves the intaglio print of the nude man. He likes to say it's better than Michelangelo's *Creation of Adam* or da Vinci's *Vitruvian Man*. Adorning the study wall, the waif frolics on a stony beach, his body half-turned to the sea. He barely looks eighteen. Our grandfather says the boy is anatomically correct. Just the right amount of muscle. We glance up at the picture, admire the striated torso, the mop of curly blond hair. The initials in the corner of the print match those of our grandfather. He doesn't know that we have seen the album locked in his drawer, the Polaroids of our grandfather as a young man. The snapshots show his attic studio, a trio of skyscrapers discernable out the window. New York, we think, or Chicago. His past life surfaces in newspaper clippings: solo shows in the 1960s, damning reviews of his out-of-vogue figurative style, the critics' names circled in red ink. The man–the boy–was the teenage son of a neighbor. An Italian family of bakers known for their Pane di Lariano and white rosettes. We imagine his name is Francesco, or something like it. He must have felt lonely in his family's house and desired to leave his parents behind. Our grandfather and Francesco must have traveled together, up and down the East Coast, finally catching a steamer to Europe. Surely they spent a summer together, in a villa overlooking the Bay of Naples. In the blue light of morning our grandfather sketched Francesco; he penciled in the contours of the boy's body, crosshatched the fall of sunlight, the shadows around his face. Those preliminary works are now lost. We have only the intaglio print. His dark eyes face the viewer: face us and our grandfather. There's a strange set of marks in the twist of his chest, a heart pushing out.

Finale

Our cellphones play an excerpt from Verdi's *Il Trovatore* at 6:37 in the mornings. We judder awake to "The Anvil Chorus," the crash of hammers striking anvil faces, again and again. Our grandfather listened to this opera every Sunday instead of going to church with our parents. By the time we had picked him up for brunch, the last act blasted from the speakers in his basement. He always said the dungeon scene was his favorite, that sometimes he too felt he was awaiting execution.

Our grandfather didn't die by an executioner's ax or by a guillotine blade slicing off his head–though he would have enjoyed the theatrically of both. He suffered a stroke soon after waking one Sunday morning. He lay in bed half-blind, his body stunned, his semi-conscious mind unaware of the blood leaking into his skull. When we discovered his cold corpse, his eyes faced the telephone on the nightstand. The handset was off the hook.

It was many years later that we realized the two of us were both using Verdi as our alarm. As twins, we were not too shocked by the coincidence. For a long time growing up, we had shared a bed and woken together to the slate-blue light of daybreak. In the short time we had alone, while our parents still slept, we pressed our heads together so hard that we could feel each other's skull. Our foreheads seemed to part, frontal bones cracked open, our brains transmitting a promise that we would never die without telling the other.

Proposal

Our patient asked us to find him a lover. He was young, twenty-two, and said he was a virgin. Or at least he felt like one. We knew most of his backstory: he snapped his neck after backflipping into a friend's swimming pool and was left wheelchair-bound, strapped into a rig of molded plastic and steel, a brace holding his spine in place, a collar keeping up his head. He told us he still felt below the belt, though we knew this was a medical impossibility. We imagined he felt his erection as a memory, the recollection of blood rushing. We had seen his penis often enough when removing the catheter from the wrinkle of skin. Our hands smelled of his vinegary urine even after we scrubbed them clean. Once he asked us to get him off. We told him we were his caregivers. We would keep him alive on our duty hours. That was it.

During the Olympics we would go to the bar and watch the bank of flat-screen televisions. He thought the televisions were futuristic and that one day we would all exist inside two-dimensional computers, free to do whatever we desired. We drank with him. Sometimes we drank too much, and we would rest our swollen feet on his footplate. When we'd leave we'd hold onto the handles, our bodies listing to one side. Weeks after the Olympics were over, he fell sick and developed a chest infection. By then he had given up on his resurrection as a digital file. We went to the bar behind the hospital, where he asked us to talk to the bartender, find him a local prostitute. Someone kind and understanding. When we spoke to the bartender, he laughed, said if he knew someone like that he would have married her. He asked if we would like to go out with him. He adored older women; they were elastic on the inside.

We took our patient out of that bar, steering him away from the gray concrete hospital where he spent so much of his time. We went to the riverside, a place rejuvenated with restaurants and galleries, and down a gravel path that overlooked the brown water. He said–and we remember this clearly–we should swim together. If we could re-teach him how to move his arms and legs, it was possible we could show him how not to drown.

When we pass the hospital now, we think of him, his chest stiffening from within, his lungs filling with fluid–our first patient who died. We often walk down to the river and think of his words. The lessons would be easy, he'd said. You've already shown me how to get in.

River

That summer, we swam across the Delaware River. We hadn't wanted to, but the woman dared us, and we were stupid young men in love with her. The filmy water churned and gurgled. On what had been the site of the lifeguard station, a wooden post stood, painted white and topped with a sign that noted the dangers of swimming. That was our point of bearing. We stripped off our white slacks and slate-blue Oxford shirts; we flung off our underwear and jumped in. The woman emitted a squeal of delight. Our thrashing strokes beat the strong current and the choppy waves, and we were sore and bruised by the time we dragged our bodies onto the far dirt bank. We were drained; we could barely stand; we glanced over to the woman on the opposite shore. She had a pink towel draped on her thin shoulders; her hair was tussled and wet. She waved at us until we stood. Somehow, she knew we weren't coming back.

Homecoming

Our motorbikes fly across the salt flats. White dust shoots up from our back tires. We twist the throttles, each of us trying to take the lead. The overhead sun beats on our shoulders, our exposed forearms, the tops of our heads. Our wraparound shades reflect the ancient lakebed, the bleached vista stretching toward the horizon. We turn the handlebars, angle now toward a wooden hut. Our trailing dust plumes swirl around, become a powdery wave. In our mirrors we watch the wave hang in midair; we like the shimmer of the floating grit, then the dissipation. The return to how things were. We increase our speed, feel salt dry our skin, sting our lips. We toss a warm beer back and forth. Our fists pump the air, and we laugh as the bottle smashes in our wake. Ahead of us heatwaves rise above the salt crust and blur the hut. A research station, one of us says. Maybe, the other thinks. Could be anything. As we get closer, less than a hundred yards away, we see the blown-out windows, the strewn plastic bottles and coolers. Then a young girl emerges; her feet appear bare and sunburnt. The girl sees us and darts inside. Another figure comes to stand in the doorway. We pull up when we realize it is a woman. She wears a dun brown coat over a calico dress, and she brandishes a tire iron. We steady our motorbikes, nod at one another when the woman retreats, and head for the hut. We careen through the doorway, wheel around, brake in front of the woman and her daughter. They guard a cooking stove, a water jug, a set of Matryoshka dolls. By a dark hole in the ground, a transistor radio plays music we don't recognize.

The woman's voice sails around us. We dismount and scoop up the girl, let her cry for a moment, then quiet; we let her whisper a welcome in our ears.

Routine

New Girl wore a knotted plaid shirt and gold lamé booty shorts. The shorts had a frilled hem and a thick, shiny waistband to collect dollar bill tips. As she bounced through the club serving drinks, we peeked, sometimes getting a hint of white butt cheek. Mostly, we saw the flesh-colored shorts she wore underneath the gold ones. She took drink orders with a slack-jawed grin. She whistled when we asked for Californian Prosecco. Then she said the bar only carries Italian.

She was smart, this New Girl. Each time we entered the club, we coaxed her over with a twenty, promised her a hundred more if she would take to the stage. She smoothed her shorts, said the fabric posed a problem: friction. We laughed, asked for our usual. She sashayed away, always brought us back two pints of domestic, maraschino cherries floating in the foam.

The other girls in the club liked to strip. They told us so. We tossed singles onto the stage, waited for New Girl to start her shift. She was always late. We imagined she took her time in the dressing room, knotting that plaid shirt, wriggling into those shorts. When she emerged we cheered, abandoned the seats in front of the stage for a back table. It wasn't long before she came our way. She told us she was quitting, leaving town for a better opportunity. We pressed our wallets into her hands. We'll make it worth your while to stay, we pleaded.

Newer Girl vaguely resembled New Girl. She wore a black bra and Daisy Dukes. Her exposed skin reminded us of New Girl's flesh-colored undershorts. We chatted with her, asked if she liked the music, the men, gold lamé. Newer Girl said she wanted to be a dancer. We knew this would never happen. She seldom smiled or brought us the right drink. She didn't even swing by our table very often; she spent most of her time watching the other girls. Each time she finished her shift, we glanced over to the staff-only door, see who would come out next.

Zia

There is part of our sister we cannot see. We trail her into the house, into her bedroom, shadow her into the boxy en-suite. She strips off her bright orange sundress, lets it drop to the marbleized vinyl floor. She glimpses the mirror and unhooks her bikini top, then fingers the bottoms. We try to look. But her pale body is turned away. We edge through the doorway. Rolls of fat rib her belly. She bends over and pulls out the scale; she stands on the platform, closes her eyes. In her moment of blindness, we sneak behind her, hide in the shower cubicle, draw the frosted curtain in front of us. Through the translucent plastic, we watch our sister peering at the dial of the scale. We see the inverse of the numbers she sees. Below her breasts, a glyph tattoo inks a section of skin: lines radiate from an invisible circle. The symbol resembles a star, but we know it is not a star. A year ago she disappeared to New Mexico, then she came back and said she had met someone in Taos. Her skin had browned. She had colorful beads twisted into her hair. She spoke of the man from the Pueblo, his stall of fry bread and clay pottery. She told us she was a stage of life ahead. Her words puzzled us. We eavesdropped on her calls, read her emails and postcards, thumbed through her texts. They talked in code; they mentioned *love* and *birth* and *running away*. We kept reading until she stopped communicating with the man, with our parents, with us. Now we pull back the curtain. We look into the center of the circle, for the hole beneath the glyph, the missing part of her, the place where our sister used to be.

Showtime

The lights in our house flare a soft red into the darkness. We crawl out from the bushes and creep along the path, make our way to the backyard. We stop at the kitchen window. Inside, our older sister climbs a stepladder, unscrews a bulb from the fixture and replaces it with a safelight. When she's down, she flips the switch. A flood of red light fills the room. She turns and heads down the hallway. We come around to the front of the house. In the living room, our sister strips off her tank top and blue jean shorts. She twirls, snaps her fingers at the window. We're sure she cannot see us – we're barely here, shadow-sisters. She presumes we're with our parents at the country club or the mall on the other side of town. She doesn't know how we enjoy her little show. Our sister jumps onto the sofa and dances, wiggles her hips, shakes her hair. In the corner of the room sits a camera mounted on a tripod. We hear the rapid whir of the shutter, see our sister's body frozen by the flash. She works through a final set of poses, playfully tugging at her pink underwear. Then she jumps down to the floor and hurries to the camera. She opens the back and removes the roll of film, sealing it in a canister. She puts the canister on top of the television and disappears to the back of the house. We sneak inside, tiptoe through the hallway, into the living room. We see our sister sorting chemical bottles in the kitchen. We take the roll of film, and slip out into the night, see what we can project upon it.

Slideshow

At one point we stood in front of the magic lantern, let the image of the Victorian-era family project onto our chests. We looked down at the painted storm clouds between our nipples and saw a father and his three children. They sat around the kitchen table, all glancing toward the window. On the other side of the pane, a silhouetted woman walked in the direction of blackened smokestacks. Beyond the factories lay a town blighted by ash-gray snow. We imagined the father cried over losing the woman. We imagined that he bent his eldest over his knee and spanked his behind. We need her, he said, hitting his son harder. Then the father's arm went slack and he watched his children hold one another. He retreated to the window: the woman was now at the factory gates talking to the foreman; the father punched the glass until the pane cracked. He cradled his hand, realizing his bloodied knuckles were broken. His children rushed away and brought back a pot of hot water and a thick cotton rag. They cleaned the blood from his fingers, then wrapped his hand with a fresh rag. As the father and his children returned to the kitchen table, the woman came back to the window and traced her finger over the broken pane and the streaks of blood. She studied the family, the man's broken hand, the glum children. She felt glad she had refused to marry the widower. She hurried away and latched onto the feathery edge of a painted cloud, swinging onto its top; the image of her vanished from our chests to somewhere beyond the beam of light.

Race

We swan dive from the rim of the crater. Warm air rushes around us, beats against our chests, slows our descent. Our friends above cheer us on, their voices echo ahead of us. Far below we can see fissures in the rock, black smoke rising in a plume. Scorching thermals blister our skin. Flakes peel off our faces, float away, back to our friends. We keep our legs together and bring our arms around to a point. Spears, each of us. Hands sharp. We speed down the throat of the volcano. We hit the billowing ash cloud and close our mouths. Silicates cut our skin, hack their way to our insides. We slip through the cloud, our bodies blessed with stigmata. The vertical channel narrows. The people at the top make bets. Both of us are longshots to live: ten to one. We fall faster, now barely able to see each other. In darkness we join hands, our upside-down bodies press together face to face, our feet lock. We surge down the tapering channel. There's still room for us, this double-spear. Sparks of light emerge from a crack far below. Rock liquefies: yellow, orange, red. A pool forms in the shape of the volcano's spine. We plunge into the magma, our skin vaporizes and our bones dissolve, our remains spread and mineralize, burst through the vent with the first eruption.

Layover

The black plume migrated with the jet stream, over islands in the Atlantic, the Labrador Sea, the vast continental landmass, to the skies above us. In the terminal, our shared wife peeks through the steel-and-glass shell, up to the artificial night sky. The source of the plume lay thousands of miles away, a volcanic stud of rock just off the coast of Iceland.

She cups her swollen belly, as though it will detach. She turns away from the darkness in front of us, says she needs a glass of water.

Particulates shimmer above the landed planes. A dance, we think. A waltz. Far more graceful than stars. We hear our wife say, Mineral, make sure it is mineral water.

The ash cloud covers the United States, masks the country from the rest of the world. Television newscasters report the closed airspace, the downed planes in Canada. They repeat the same details until the stations flicker to static. We touch the glass wall in front of us. Silver-gray flakes speckle the surface. We can feel the cold, the creep through our fingertips. A knot of vapor descends from the bottom of the plume. Little curls tail off, bring the cloud along.

Our wife gripes about her throat. I can taste the air, she says.

We tell ourselves we will help her in a moment, once the chill inside of us has passed.

Out on the tarmac, a commercial airliner turns on its lights. White beams blink into the terminal. We are blinded. We collapse to the polished tile floor; our knuckles press against the glass. Jet engines roar outside, then stutter, die. Once nightfall shrouds the airport, a woman appears on the runway, in the last layer of clear air. She crawls on her hands and knees toward the now-dark plane, her belly scraping the ground. She cries our unborn daughter's name. The ash cloud swallows her, and her inside, takes them away.

Terminal

We left her silver-chain pendant at the airport. It was always better not to carry physical reminders of dead relatives. We had once read this piece of advice in a women's magazine as we waited for a routine procedure. The dentist was removing our old mercury fillings; he told us they were poisonous, that breathing mercury vapor could lead to stroke or crippling brain disease. He informed us we would not remember who other people were; we would not even recognize the faces of our parents or children. Prosopagnosia, he said. Unless we replaced our old fillings, we would be neurologically impaired for the rest of our lives. In the years since this warning, we have wished for neurological impairment to help us forget our grandmother dying of endometrial cancer. Her death-face had stiffened her jaw, thinned her scraggly gray hair. Her lids were slightly open, the sclera of her eyes a sickly yellow. We took her silver pendant before they carted her away on the gurney. We ran the silver chain through our fingers, passing it back and forth, sister to sister. The amethyst sat in a cheap setting. We knew it was worth only a few dollars. It didn't mean much sentimentally either. Our grandmother had purchased it from a pawn shop a few months before her death. Yet, the glint in the purple stone held something of our grandmother, too much for us to carry it around. Before we boarded the plane back to our children, our normal lives, we hung the pendant around the neck of a female mannequin, a face we would never recognize again.

This

She posts online: racial diatribes, anti-feminist manifestos, inter-species videos, especially ones documenting the special friendships of raccoons and parrots. All night she shares and comments, unfriends strangers and ex-colleagues, then adds us, our shared account. Her posts rant, misspell everything–orangge, poltikal, pheotus–quote Wikipedia, White Power sites. She shills MLM night creams, juice cleanses, colorful vitamin powders; she shows before and after pictures–her products good for insomnia, sun damage, breast cancer. We receive her event invitations, pages to Like, links to sites on the Dark Web. We ignore them all. We sit in front of the screen, transfixed by her actions. We suspect she is a bot or a troll or a syndicate of viral marketing professionals. Undoubtedly she lives in Moscow or Pyongyang or New Jersey. She must be a white man, or desires to be: she posts denials about Auschwitz, rages about the New World Order and the Masonic symbols on the dollar bill. Then her conspiracy chatter disappears. She creates an album: "Dead Child." We watch her follower count shrink. We hesitate. We almost block her. Uploaded Polaroids appear–three Christmas snapshots, years apart, all capturing a small blond boy. He ages from a swaddled baby to a brat stealing a look at his presents. The final image ages him to a stern teen. In camo pajamas, he clutches his longbow and hunting knife, the blade pressed against his wrist. She asks us to report the images as abusive, as harmful content, adults only. Before we can respond, the pictures blink away. Everything is gone, save one message on her page: *Tell me where you are?*

Memes

We embed Wonka in the cold electric of the screen. We should call him a chocolatier. Man of confection. He produces sugared candies with sleight of hand, cranking out each one with a mechanical device of vacuum tubes and copper kettles. We have never seen him do this. We have only viewed his picture online. An oblong border imprisons his upper torso, and his cocksure face rests on his knuckles. He wears a purple velour jacket, a bowtie of Bourbon influence, and a top hat from which his blond curls spill out. We look to him as a stand-in for our father. The man who left us and went to Florida. The man who said he had to find himself. Find out what had happened to his life, his younger spirit. We remember the forearm of the young woman in his Camaro–the tanned length of flesh that rested on the doorframe; the downy hair; the fingers clutching a vial of Klonopin. Then our father drove away.

Now we create new memes and write slurs in the caption boxes. All night we deface our father's universe with pithy phrases, sentence fragments, put-downs of TV celebrities, digs at our mother. She is in the next room, watching cable, drinking the last of her malt liquor. Annular pustules star her body, and she cradles her stomach and imagines the coming months. She does not cruise the bars anymore. She has too much sadness and she aches in her joints and in the part of her head where she loves us. She pretends not to think about our father or our old lives or the echocardiogram of an arrhythmic fetal heart. But she tells us again and again our father has another son. We had assumed he was penisless, like the Pied Piper and his metonymic flute. It is hard to ignore his baby. He has an entourage of six polygons. He exudes *joie de vivre* while giving *joie de vivre* the finger. His polygon friends make his fat face dynamic and angry. We hate his pep, his infantile superiority. The *fuck you* is a *fuck you* directed at us. There are too many similarities to our father's letter. He used stationary from a Howard Johnson outside of Atlanta–his halfway point to New Smyrna–and wrote us a single paragraph of apologetic clichés and vague statements on the nature of paternal love. The text had been printed under an image of a blue motor lodge and the words, "The Flavor of America." For years we analyzed the meaning of the phrase, whether he chose it deliberately or whether it was the first scrap of paper he found after inseminating his new girlfriend. Since then we have grown into cartoon teenagers, with spiked red hair and pink gelatinous skin. We know our father works as a security guard at an outlet mall and his girlfriend rents a sunglasses kiosk at the same place. We know he returns our mail. We know he thinks about us. We know. We know. We know. We follow him on Twitter and Instagram, repeatedly Friend him on Facebook, dial him anonymously through Skype. When he answers and says *Eric Miller here*, in the third-person, we terminate the connection. We are skeptical of the way things have changed. We exist more online. Our thoughts center on how to escape, how to begin again. Part of us is in the electric ether, or so we dream. We are envious of a version of ourselves a thousand years in the future, looking back, wondering how everything is de-atomized into pixels, pulses of light and energy.

Chorus

We only sing in unison for those we hate. The length of that list of people weighs on us, begs us to winnow down to those who matter. For years, our parents lugged us to psychiatric specialists, one doctor after another. These doctors–always men–offered us a host of panaceas. Usually, their cure-alls came in the form of medication: chlorpromazine, trifluoperazine, even ziprasidone. Always, they required follow-up sessions, our parents noting the list of dates. When the treatments failed, we were referred to noted experts–tailor-suited men, gray at the temples, faces tan from Caribbean sun or red from Speyside Scotch–who considered us through thick spectacles. They asked questions about our sexual histories, the frequency of our masturbation. We lied to them, offered potted histories of hook-ups with fellow high schoolers and science teachers, and Math Club coaches. Sometimes, when we wanted a reaction, we named our friends and described our acts of cunnilingus for as long as the doctors could take it. Unknown to our parents, several of the doctors propositioned us: a harmless coffee, a drink, soda if you want, an invitation to a lake house or afternoon in a hotel room–a five-star, they always noted. In our eighteenth year, we left home, left behind the litany of specialists, our collection of orange pill vials. We slipped across the state line, declaring that we were glad to be free. We drove all night. The sun rose over the cornfields, illuminated the wind turbines, and our ears were soon alert to the hum of the blades. We flipped on the radio, sang along to whatever music the stations played. Our car slowed through the foothills, crawled along the mountain roads. When we hit the coast, the salt air stung our throats, and we bounced inland to L.A., slept in our car in West Hollywood, couchsurfed in Pasadena, then found a sublet in The Valley. We shacked up with an older couple, the woman a phone-sex operator with an aversion to natural light. Black bags were taped to the windows; she proclaimed her love for perpetual twilight, never for her boyfriend. She worked all night, smoking pot and drinking vodka lemonades until she could no longer comment on her wetness. Once, when she fell asleep on her suede couch, we took a call. We rasped an old country song and the man on the other end hung up. We sang hymn lyrics to the next caller, a Scottish ballad to the one after that. Finally, on an Auto-Tuned pop hit, a male voice told us we were awful. After that we signed up for singing lessons, learning to control our vocals and harmonize. We karaoked on weeknights, graduating months later to club performances for a few dollars a show. We drank every night, slept with every man or woman who wanted us. Our bodies bruised, became infected, suffered through venereal disease. To recover, we fled to a farming town in the Midwest, joined a church and sometimes prayed. Once in a while, we still sneaked into the cornfields at dusk. In the graying light, we whispered to the turbines: *We will never forgive.* It took years of prayer to make a difference. We chose not to reconcile, but to forget: to cross those people off we could barely remember. Hate is such a strong word. The list of names now stands at only two.

Counterpoint

What is it to be *I* versus *we*?

One of the axioms we have gleaned concerns the plurality of nature. Everything exists in more than one form–the hand, for example, repeated *ad infinitum* through the primate line. From the *Carlito syrichta* to the *Chlorocebus aethiops* we see these fleshy appendages of nerved muscle and bone. Variations on a theme. Twins, for most people, seem to be nature's exception. Whatever mirror image strangers see in us, we know the aberrations between our bodies.

Recently we have been thinking about those people from long ago: our parents. They were teachers, of a sort. They raised us in the Northwest, on a property line that straddled two states. We remember the logging road that ran up to our childhood home. Thick pine flanked the sides of the cabin, a mat of needles crowned the roof; a tuft of moss encircled the tin chimney pipe, black smoke corkscrewing into the air. Sometimes, we would sit on the roof and huff the smoke, breathe out wisps, half-choke, blacken our lungs. Our heads would spin, our eyes water, but the worse was the prickle in our throats, the eruption of vomit over the side of the roof. Our mother would scold us. Each time we climbed down and stood in front of her, she grabbed our arms, dragged us inside, shoved us to our knees. She pressed her thumbs against our closed eyes. The pressure, she said, reset the behavioral section of our brains.

At night, in our shared bed, we signed our secret language. We touched each other's palms with a series of taps and swirls of our fingertips, using pauses as punctuation. We mulled over our mother's words. She believed we should be like her, part of the family unit–which, really, was our father's cabal. He marooned us, said homeschool would teach us everything we needed to know. His oft-repeated sermon on the degenerate art of Michelangelo usually devolved into misrepresentation of men's lives: homosexuals should never be fathers.

Once, when our father crossed the property line for a supply run, we skulked out of the back of the cabin. Our mother called after us. We charged into the forest, making our way through the sprawl of pine and fir. We spent the first night shivering on a bed of moss, the second holding each other by the river. Eventually we found a dirt road and thumbed our way out of the state, hitched a ride with some farmhands heading south for work in Texas. We lay in the bed of the truck, hidden beneath a stiff tarp. We heard one of the men explain he was from Michigan, the town of Port Austin, near the top of his thumb.

We pulled into a truck stop. Some of the men were headed to Abilene, the driver to Corpus Christi. We wanted to see water, oceans that led to places beyond our country. Inside the diner, we talked with truckers about routes to Mexico. They hawed about transporting us across the border. They shook our hands and wished us luck. Outside, we watched the traffic thunder past. Our logger rides were heading in different directions. We unclasped our hands, a temporary goodbye, allowed our minds to separate: to think I and I.

And I.

I.

Disconnected

We came to the hotel to end it all. The building sat tucked in the mountains, part of an Edwardian-era resort. Gentlemen and women used to enjoy the crisp air for a few weeks, then exalt the health benefits back to their friends in the city. All those people, we realized, were long dead.

We had traveled thousands of miles and we sat now in a room in an abandoned hotel. Winter sun lit up the furred ice on the pane. We bent over the desk in front of the window, our fingers dancing over the pleather inlay. One of us brought out a copy of *The Enneads* and creased it open to the final section. We had last read Plotinus in a public library in L.A. some years ago. We had studied his Theory of Forms, though understood little of it, save that men and women were indivisible: *atoma eidē*. We had an innate sense that we were true forms, pure, models for the universe, for our parents, for our lost friends, for all those who had intersected our lives.

Now we were far from anyone who knew us. Outside, snow flurried across the hills and down to the river. We could see a faint reflection of ourselves in the glass; we hardly recognized the blurred faces that stared back. We felt adrift. Tangled and untangled. There was little left for us in the world.

We used the room's old rotary telephone to call the men who knew our mother; all the numbers we could remember. Voices castigated us. They vented at our intrusion, our prying questions. We didn't care; we wanted to know which of the men was our father.

The men hung up in salvos of *fuck off* and *wrong number* and *leave me alone* and *I don't know you.*

In the dark we lit votive candles, then rolled onto the bed and wrapped ourselves in the sheets. We discussed what had come before and what was still to come. Our brief time apart had shown us we had to separate from each other more permanently. The strongest of us took the handset and looped the cord around our necks, coils tightening against our tracheas.

As children, we were told that we had been part of a multiple. In our mother's womb there were several of us, at least five competing heartbeats that faded to four, then three. The final two felt forever conjoined: a single person masquerading as twins, sometimes triplets.

An individual who would never accept they were alone.

At some point late in the night, I heard the mechanical ring of the telephone. The pleasing sound reverberated around the room. Then the phones in the other bedrooms rang, hundreds of them singing together, a chorus. I reached for the handset and pressed it to my ear; I knew it would be my mother; she would tell me to come home.

Acknowledgments

Thanks to the advice and support of James Brubaker, Suzi Eckl, Toni Graham, James Tate Hill, Rachel Klammer, Richard Peabody, Melissa Richer, Ashley Wilson, Keith York, Oliver Zarandi, and to Courtney Sender for her invaluable editing. Thanks also to the institutional support of the Vermont Studio Center, the Ragdale Foundation, and the Virginia Center for the Creative Arts. And finally my gratitude to Guy Bennett and the MFA students of Otis College.

I am grateful to the editors of the following journals in which these stories first appeared:

"Chorus" *Hotel Amerika*
"Counterpoint" *The Vassar Review*
"Lecture" *The Coe Review*
"This" *Sierra Nevada Review*
"Recoil" *Nebo*
"Memes" *Funhouse*
"Visitation" *The New Territory*
"Initiation" SAND
"Reunion" *Gargoyle*
"The Temple" *Big Lucks*
"Procedure" and "Ceremony" *Flash: The International Short-Short Story Magazine*
"Zia" *Map Literary*
"Gestalt" *Grub Street*
"Rope Trick" *Bending Genres*
"Cul-de-Sac" and "Dinner" X-R-A-Y *Literary Magazine*
"Slideshow" *Litro*
"Terminal" *Ghost Parachute*
"Belief" *New World Writing*
"Directory" *Swamp Ape Review*
"Proposal" *Meridian*

"Finale" *Whale Road Review*
"Masterpiece" *Atticus Review*
"Pitstop" and "Routine" *Big Muddy*
"Apocrypha" *Popshot*
"Timber" *Café Irreal*
"Disconnected" *Heavy Feather Review*
"Date Night" *Oyster River Pages*

Christopher Linforth has recently published work in *The Millions, Fiction International, Epiphany, Notre Dame Review, Day One, Hotel Amerika,* and *Descant,* among other magazines. He has been awarded fellowships and scholarships to The Sewanee Writers' Conference, Vermont Studio Center, and The Virginia Center for the Creative Arts.

Other Titles from Otis Books

Erik Anderson, *The Poetics of Trespass*
J. Reuben Appelman, *Make Loneliness*
Renée Ashley, *Ruined Traveler*
Guy Bennett, *Self-Evident Poems*
Guy Bennett and Béatrice Mousli, Editors, *Seeing Los Angeles: A Different Look at a Different City*
Steve Castro, *Blue Whale Phenomena*
Geneva Chao, *one of us is wave one of us is shore*
Robert Crosson, *Signs / & Signals: The Daybooks of Robert Crosson*
———, *Daybook (1983–86)*
Neeli Cherkovski and Bill Mohr, Editors, *Cross-Strokes: Poetry between Los Angeles and San Francisco*
Mohammed Dib, *Tlemcen or Places of Writing*
Ray DiPalma, *The Ancient Use of Stone: Journals and Daybooks, 1998–2008*
———, *Obedient Laughter*
François Dominique, *Solène*
Tim Erickson, *Egopolis*
Jean-Michel Espitallier, *Espitallier's Theorem*
Forrest Gander, Editor, *Panic Cure: Poems from Spain for the 21st Century*
Van G. Garrett, *Water Bodies*
Leland Hickman, *Tiresias: The Collected Poems of Leland Hickman*
Michael Joyce, *Twentieth Century Man*
Lew S. Klatt, *The Wilderness After Which*
Norman M. Klein, *Freud in Coney Island and Other Tales*
Alan Loney, *Beginnings*
Luxorius, *Opera Omnia or, a Duet for Sitar and Trombone*
Sara Marchant, *Proof of Loss*
Ken McCullough, *Left Hand*
Gary McDowell, *Cæsura: Essays*
Béatrice Mousli, Editor, *Review of Two Worlds: French and American Poetry in Translation*
Laura Mullen, *Enduring Freedom*
Ryan Murphy, *Down with the Ship*
Mostafa Nissabouri, *For an Ineffable Metrics of the Desert*
Aldo Palazzeschi, *The Arsonist*
Dennis Phillips, *Navigation: Selected Poems, 1985–2010*

Antonio Porta, *Piercing the Page: Selected Poems 1958–1989*
Eric Priestley, *For Keeps*
Sophie Rachmuhl, *A Higher Form of Politics: The Rise of a Poetry Scene, Los Angeles, 1950–1990*
Dorothy Rice, *Gray Is the New Black*
Norberto Luis Romero, *The Obscure Side of the Night*
Olivia Rosenthal, *We're Not Here to Disappear*
Noah Ross, *Swell*
Amelia Rosselli, *Hospital Series*
———, *War Variations*
Ari Samsky, *The Capricious Critic*
Giovanna Sandri, *only fragments found: selected poems, 1969–1998*
Hélène Sanguinetti, *Hence This Cradle*
Janet Sarbanes, *Army of One*
Severo Sarduy, *Beach Birds*
Adriano Spatola, *The Porthole*
———, *Toward Total Poetry*
Billie R. Tadros, *The Tree We Planted and Buried You In*
Carol Treadwell, *Spots and Trouble Spots*
Paul Vangelisti, *Wholly Falsetto with People Dancing*
Paul Vangelisti & Dennis Phillips, *Mapping Stone*
Allyssa Wolf, *Vaudeville*
